Creative Writi

Amanda J Harrington

Contents

Introduction

Creative Writing for Teens is part of the Creative Writing for Kids series. This series brings out the fun in creative writing and literacy, helping young people to develop **creative thinking** and gain a sense of achievement as well as **new skills**.

All the chapters in Creative Writing for Teens are separate but working through them gradually builds skills, preparing young writers for the more complex sections later in the book. By the end of the book, young people have achieved a full creative literacy workout.

Creative Writing for Teens enables young people to break out of the traditional, structured story-writing process often imposed in schools, giving them the skills and ambition to think of their own, **original ideas** and exploring how these can be used.

The exercises and activities within this book are based around set **scenarios**, sometimes detailed, sometimes more fluid, and then a **task** or **questions** which lead to a wholly original piece of work.

Each chapter in the book is split into sections and tasks so that work can be completed in stages and each idea is fully explored. There is a full set of work and ideas within each section, giving a good understanding of different topics. This also means the book can be picked up whenever needed, without having to do lots of work all at once.

The creative work in this book is a combination of **practical/technical exercises**, such as working on leaflets and reports and imaginative writing with exciting and gripping **story ideas**. All the work is **fully guided** with lots of example answers, leading up to the Klamarty Caves chapter at the end which blends the practical with the mysterious in a **long, detailed and immersive project**.

Advice is given throughout the book, as well as clear example answers and partial stories. Young people are not left to think of everything themselves, they are **supported** as they work. Enthusiastic writers can extend the work (there are suggestions for extra activities) and those who find creative writing more difficult can work at their own pace without feeling pressured to give the 'right' answer.

All the exercises have been used in **real-life tuition** and classes, with **different ages and abilities**, by students aged **13 to 19**.

This book can be paired with **Creative Literacy: English GCSE** by Amanda J Harrington.

1.1 Tumbleweed Mansion: Introduction

In this section you will be visiting old Tumbleweed Mansion, using descriptive work, plans, scenarios, character and storyline creation.

Read the scenario below then work your way through the tasks. When you have to choose between different outcomes, try writing about more than one result so that you can explore what might happen.

Scenario

The old estate of Tumbleweed has been empty for more than ten years. The last owner lived there, using only one room. The rest of the big, graceful mansion was left to fall into ruin.

The mansion is much-loved by locals as there is a right of way across the grounds which connects the town with a beautiful stretch of countryside a couple of miles away. Also, the old owner used to let the townspeople hold events on the land around the mansion so many locals have happy memories of summer picnics, fairs and carnivals taking place there.

Now Tumbleweed is for sale and there are quite a few interested buyers. Local people are worried about who will buy Tumbleweed. Will it be spoiled or can it be saved?

1.2 Tumbleweed Mansion: The Plans

Scenario

Imagine you are the estate agent managing the sale of the mansion. You need to make it seem attractive and a good prospect, even though it might take years and lots of money to repair it.

Read the facts below, study the plans for the ground floor and then move onto the tasks to see if you can sell the mansion.

Important Facts

The mansion started life as a simple merchant's house and was extended in Victorian times.

The grounds are split into an acre of formal gardens (now grown wild) and ten acres of fields, currently being used by a local farmer to feed his cows.

The sale of the mansion includes rights to fish in the river running through the grounds.

Features in the mansion date back to the 17th century, such as the patterned tiles in the main hall and the wood carvings in the formal dining room.

There is a very big hole in the back of the roof and bats have moved in.

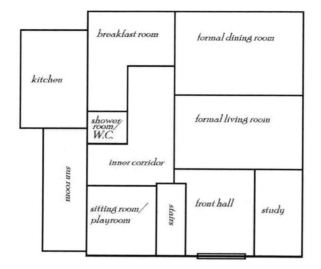

Tumbleweed Mansion
ground floor

Task 1: The rooms

Look at the basic plans for the ground floor of the mansion. Decide where doors, windows and any extras like cupboards should be placed. Rooms are set out for you, so think about how these connect.

Room sizes

Draw the doors, windows etc onto the plan and label the rooms with sizes (in feet or metres). (If you like, scan the plans and print them out before drawing on them).

Your room sizes don't have to be very accurate, you just need an idea of how big the mansion is compared to a normal house. If in doubt, measure the room you are in first and then decide how big the mansion's rooms might be.

Upstairs

Now draw your own version of the plans for the upstairs. Decide how many bedrooms there will be plus any extra rooms such as a nursery or an upstairs study or sitting room. Will there be an old balcony or stairs to the attic? And how many bathrooms will there be?

Task 2: The Layout

Write a full description of the mansion's layout, based on the plan and your own ideas. A good way to do this is to imagine you are walking through the mansion, explaining as you go which rooms lead where and whether there are any special features.

This is the point where you should really begin to think about what the mansion might look like, inside and out. Describing it will bring it to life for you and will also help you visualise Tumbleweed's future, in the rest of this section.

Pictures

Decide which pictures you would take to include with the property details and explain what the pictures would show. Use at least 5 (imaginary) pictures.

You don't need to draw the pictures (though you can if you want). Describe what each one would show; for instance, one might be the front of the mansion, taken so that you couldn't see the broken windows on the left hand side.

Pictures are very important when selling any kind of property but would be essential with Tumbleweed Mansion as it is so different from other buildings. To encourage people to visit, you need to make it look attractive.

You might also include:

Picture/s which show the potential of the land, such as how big the grounds are or the river with fishing rights.

Include a picture of the local town to explain how close the mansion is, making it more attractive to businesses or property developers.

Images of original features to persuade people the mansion can be restored.

A view of the largest rooms, for any businesses which might need big spaces for functions.

1.3 Tumbleweed Mansion: Sell, sell, sell!

Task 1: The Details

Write the property details as they will appear in the estate agent's window. This is different from simply describing the layout and any special features – it should be **persuasive** and make people want to view the mansion.

Be positive but try not to tell lies about the mansion! How will you avoid making it sound like a ruin? Will you mention the hole in the roof?

Estate agents tend to focus on the positive and minimise negative features so the hole in the roof could become 'needs some renovation' and the massively overgrown gardens could be 'waiting to be restored to their former glory'. This is far better than saying the roof is a money pit and the gardens would need a team of goats to break through the weeds.

Tip: Try writing a set of details which are objective and honest, mentioning the faults just as they are without trying to hide them. Once you have done this it becomes easier to look at your own writing and change the negative areas to more positive language and change the objective, honest descriptions to more persuasive language.

Look at my two examples to help you see the difference. The first example tells the complete truth and the second one changes it to sound more positive. I have concentrated on the kitchen.

Example Details

Honest: *The kitchen will need full renovation before it can be used. We recommend re-plastering the whole room and new windows are necessary. The pantry will need to be knocked down and could become part of the kitchen. The cooker is unsafe and should be removed by a qualified tradesman.*

Positive: *The kitchen would benefit from professional re-modelling, including plaster work. Some attention is needed on the windows but they offer a lovely view out to the side gardens where they originally showed a corner of the herb garden. The pantry could become part of the whole kitchen, opening up the space to create a large family area. The cooker will need replaced but there is mains gas to the property.*

Task 2: The newspaper advert

Write a shortened version of your property details as an advert for the local paper. This should also be positive but only include the main points.

This is a shorter version than your other descriptions but needs to grab the attention of potential buyers as they read the newspaper, so the language used should be direct and persuasive. I have provided some phrases to help you but you can use your own instead or as well as these.

Your advert would usually be a picture of the main house with a heading to draw the readers in, then simplified description beneath – all phrased in a positive, sales-pitch way.

Try writing two versions of the advert, a short one and a longer, feature advert which would be placed at the top of the property pages.

Phrases

Local beauty spot

Massive potential

Wonderful views

Wealth of original features

Amazing restoration project

Once-in-a-lifetime opportunity

1.4 Tumbleweed Mansion: The Buyers

Read the descriptions of the buyers who are interested in Tumbleweed Mansion. Each one has positive and negative aspects which would affect the future of the old mansion.

The Property Developer

Greg Yurt is a local property developer. He wants to make the mansion into a large estate with the mansion building turned into lots of one bedroom flats and then executive houses being built in the grounds.

Greg has the money and experience to carry out his plans and is used to getting his own way.

As part of his plan, he would offer some of the flats to local people at reduced prices. He would also landscape and manage the grounds as a communal area for people living on the new estate. People who buy his new properties will also be able to fish in the river.

The Local

Barry Crane lives in a little row of houses with a view over the mansion and its grounds. He has watched the old mansion grow more unloved and wants to save it. He thinks it would make a great community building for the whole town where businesses, local groups and a myriad of community events could bring everyone together.

He has no money to buy the mansion but he has lots of plans and has managed to gain the support of two local businesses who have promised to lend him money. If he can gather enough support, perhaps he would have enough to buy the mansion.

He plans to keep the mansion grounds as close to their original design as possible, as well as hosting local events like when he was a child.

The Designer

Felicity Brown grew up in the village and moved away when she started earning lots of money with her interior design business. Now she wants to buy the mansion and have it as a holiday home a few weeks a year, letting it out to high-class tourists the rest of the time.

She is willing to renovate the whole building and be faithful to its original charm and period features. She wants to make sure the right of way is closed off as her guests would not appreciate locals tramping over the grounds. She would also grass over the whole of the grounds as plants are a bit untidy, you know.

The Team-builder

Tom Pendlebury has never heard of Tumbleweed Mansion before but thinks it would make the perfect venue for his team-building business. He would renovate the building, ripping out all the original features and make it a set of good quality, hotel-style rooms with the downstairs being converted into a commercial kitchen and conference room. He would run activities inside and outside, including paint-balling and competitive trampolining.

He is more than happy to keep the right of way and would also employ local people to help him run the place.

1.5 Tumbleweed Mansion: The Perfect Buyer?

Scenario

Who should buy the mansion? Is it better to keep the mansion and lose all the original features? Should people have the new homes a property developer would bring? Should someone like Felicity buy it so that it can be renovated to its original state?

Each of the buyers has positive aspects they would bring to the mansion and some would also be good for the local area but none of them are without their faults.

Task

One by one, explain the **benefits and disadvantages** of each potential buyer. Be objective, so that even if you feel one person would be very bad for the mansion or the local area, try to explain their good points as a buyer.

You should include:

Positives and negatives of each buyer

Besides Barry, which buyer might be the most popular with local people and why?

What might each buyer mean for the long-term future of the mansion and its grounds? For instance, would Felicity end up selling the mansion at some stage? Would Barry be able to pay the running costs every year, as well as finding the money to buy it in the first place?

1.6 Tumbleweed Mansion: A Plea or Two

Scenario 1

Barry writes a heartfelt piece for the local newspaper explaining why he wants to buy the mansion and what it would bring to the local community. He is impassioned and enthusiastic in his support for the mansion as a community centre. If belief and energy were all it took, then Barry would already have the mansion!

Task 1

Write the newspaper piece for Barry, being as persuasive and emotive as possible.

You should include:

Lots of emotive language – remember, Barry cares deeply about the mansion but is not a businessman

Descriptions of how the mansion was in the past and how the community used to meet there

Descriptions of how it might be used in the future

A small mention of where the money will come from to buy and fund the mansion (but do not spend much time on this as Barry isn't really sure where the money is coming from).

Scenario 2

Greg responds by writing his own piece for the newspaper. He is not emotional and wants people to see how much sense it makes to create new homes from an old ruin. Although his argument is based on logic, he is still determined to win people over and get his own way.

Task 2

Write Greg's piece to the newspaper. Decide whether you want to make it persuasive, argumentative or both.

You should include:

Why he wants to buy the mansion, in his own words

What he would bring to the local area

Why local support is important to him (it might not be important to him but he wants people to be on his side)

Think about the language he would choose. He believes money is the driving factor and will want people to know he has the money to make his plans work and also that it might be good for them, financially

1.7 Tumbleweed Mansion: The Leaflet

Scenario

Tom has been interviewing for jobs at his new team-building centre and he hasn't even bought the mansion yet! He is so confident in his bid to buy the mansion that he has also written and produced the leaflet to go with his new team-building centre.

Task

Write Tom's leaflet for the mansion, as if he has bought it and it has become his centre. You can either just write the text for the leaflet or also design the leaflet itself to wrap around your text.

You should include:

The name of his team-building centre

The best features of this new centre

Any connections it has to the local area

Activities on offer at the centre

A short description of the grounds and the local area

1.8 Tumbleweed Mansion: Who Wins?

Scenario

Who will win the battle to buy Tumbleweed Mansion?

Will you choose your favourite buyer or the one who will be the best for the mansion? Or will it be whoever came up with the right money?

Task 1

Decide who will be the successful buyer and write about their success in the form of a **story**. Will there be any surprises?

You should include:

How they managed to beat the other buyers

What they do with it in the end

Task 2

It has been three years since Tumbleweed Mansion was bought and transformed into a new life. Describe what has happened in those years and how it all turned out in the end. Did it all go to plan?

2.1 Sharing a Personality: Who I Am

Scenario

In this exercise, you are going to explore your own personality and then use it in an inventive way to create a completely new character. Be as honest as possible when answering the questions and completing the tasks. You can keep this work to yourself, without showing it to anyone, so feel free to reveal your whole personality.

Firstly, work through these tasks which help you to describe yourself.

Task 1: In My Own Words

What are your **main** personality features? Think of how you can describe yourself in a few sentences. Be honest! Don't just write about your love of animals or kindness to your fellow humans; also include your ability to vanish when there is hard work to be done.

Task 2: The Secret Side of Me

What side to your personality do most people not get to see? What is there about your personality that might surprise others? You might be very loud at school then come home to groom guinea pigs for rodent shows.

Write about a secret side of you, something that either no one knows about or only your closest friends and family see in you.

If you find this difficult, think about an aspect of your personality that you would not be happy talking about in a school assembly.

Task 3: What I Like to Do

Think of an activity or everyday event which shows your personality. Describe it in detail and explain why it suits your personality.

You could include something you do all the time, like playing football with your friends. This would show you as a sociable person who enjoyed team games. Or you could describe how you come home and like to spend time in your room, playing on the computer. This would help to describe how you are quieter and don't need people around you all the time.

You could also include a more out-of-the-ordinary activity which would suit your personality, such as scuba diving to show you are adventurous, or busking in the middle of town, to show you are creative and also brave!

Task 4: Who I Might Be

Now describe yourself as if you were talking about a **fictional character**. You can either write this as part of a story or make it a standard description with full sentences.

Think of everything you have discussed so far and include it in your description. If you like, you can give yourself another name to make it easier to write about yourself.

Example

Karl liked to go out with his friends, knocking on doors and running away. He knew it was wrong but loved the buzz of excitement when they were nearly caught.

2.2 Sharing a Personality: Who Do You Think I Am?

Scenario

Your friends and family feel they know you best but sometimes our friends see us differently than our family might. It doesn't mean you are being fake or false with your friends, just that you show them another part of your personality than the one your family knows.

Task 1: Friends and Family

Describe yourself through the eyes of your **friends** and then the eyes of your **family**, either as a list or short sentences. Think of as many words or phrases as you can because they will be useful for the rest of this section.

Task 2: My Friend

Now choose one friend and pretend they are talking about you. How would they describe you if they were talking to someone else? Imagine the other person had never met you. What words and phrases would your friend choose to make sure they described you perfectly?

Task 3: My Family

Think of a family member who is the most likely to boast about you, someone who will sound your praises and tell everyone they know when you do something good.

From their point of view, boast about yourself! Use real-life events or make some up and talk about yourself in glowing terms. Use positively over-the-top language.

2.3 Sharing a Personality: Who I Might Have Been

Scenario

Now think about where the different traits of your personality came from. You might automatically think of your parents, but I want you to go much further back than that.

Imagine you could meet a relative from the past. They are very much like you in personality but their **lifestyle** is completely different.

This is almost like thinking of yourself living life in the past. Imagine your relative as someone who is very much like you but is still a separate person.

Task 1: Your relative

Think about your relative from the past. Decide how far back you want to go and who they might be.

Give them a name, age and choose the period of history they are from. Also include any relevant details of their life.

Now write about them, describing them as if they are a real person. Use my example to help you.

Example

This is Marie. She is a young girl in the 16th century who has come over from France with her father. She is settling into a new town and learning to speak English so she can make friends.

Marie is very shy and likes to stay at home. She needs to go out a lot to help her father and to look for work but she would rather read books in their quiet little study.

Marie likes to laugh but often finds it hard to relax with new people. She is starting to make friends with the merchant's daughter where her father buys his supplies. The other girl is much louder than Marie but they enjoy trying to understand each other.

Do you see how you can make up a completely new character but have them share aspects of your personality? To make it more natural, you can include details from their life which don't have anything to do with their personality – such as Marie having to go to the merchant with her father.

Task 2: A surprise

Now you are going to describe a scene where your long-lost relative encounters something surprising. This can be a nice or nasty surprise or even something terrifying.

Consider how they would react to the unexpected. Remember to imagine how *you* would react, as their personality is based on your own.

Here are some examples to get you started. Feel free to use your own ideas instead.

Someone breaks into the house

There is the sound of drums in the distance

Something precious is broken

The lock is stuck!

They have discovered a secret

The animals have escaped

A wonderful present

Someone is hiding

Going on holiday

Task 3: Opposites

Imagine your relative has to stay with someone from their family who is their direct opposite in personality. How would they react? Would they get along? How would you react if this happened to you?

1. Write a short description of the new person. Include details of how they are different from your relative.

2. Describe a scene from your relative's stay with this other person. You should show how they are different, describing how they interact and the kind of relationship they have. Use my example to help you.

Example

Marie could not stand another moment with Uncle Benjamin in the house. He shouted at night when he was drunk and then shouted in the morning when she made noise as she did the housework. He was unpleasant and rude and only seemed to get along with her father.

Do you see how you can describe someone's personality by explaining what they **do**? Rather than just saying Benjamin was loud, I said he shouted when he was drunk, which tells us he is loud without having to state the obvious.

3.1 School Times: The Stories

Scenario

You have taken over the job of running the school newspaper. This newspaper has never been more than a couple of sheets of information, sometimes with pictures for big events. You want to transform it into a proper newspaper but have only been given two days to do the first edition.

You spend the first day tracking down and exploring stories, news, events and anything else you might be able to include in the newspaper.

Due to shortness of time, you can only use **5 stories** and two choices are already taken with stories the Head has told you to include.

Stories

Story 1 (you must include this one)

The facts: Jessica Evanson is going to be made head girl again. She has only missed being head girl one year in her whole school life and that was because she moved to France for six months, so wasn't actually in school.

The story: This story will feature a gleaming picture of Jessica in all her perfection. Decide on the tone of your story – will you be supportive about her being head girl or will you reveal her as the terror of Year 10?

Story 2

The facts: Barry the school tortoise has disappeared again. During your investigations you make the shocking discovery that Barry is the third school tortoise and has been replaced the other times he disappeared! You don't know what happened to the other tortoises but this could be a big story. You have been warned off investigating by the Deputy Head.

The story: You have the choice to investigate more and find out what happened to Barrys 1 and 2 or feature the story as it stands and let the school know they have been deceived. You risk getting into trouble with the Deputy Head but you could make that part of the story.

Story 3 (You must include this one)

The facts: The new school menu has gone live and with it the cafeteria has emptied. The food is very healthy but either tastes really bad or doesn't taste of anything at all. You have been instructed to write a **positive** piece about the new menu as the local mayor is coming to try a meal in a few days' time.

The story: This story should include at least two descriptions of new meals on offer. Find a way to describe the new menu honestly while keeping it as positive as possible. Can you do both?

Story 4

The facts: There is a strange tapping noise on the second floor of building

B on school grounds. This is known as the Ghost of B. As far as you can tell, the ghost story has been around for at least 4 years. You don't believe in ghosts but the noise is very real – even the teachers are a bit nervous of working up there. Your investigations have turned up the interesting fact that every time the caretaker has been sent to sort out the noise, he has come back drunk.

The story: This story should feature an interview with the caretaker, either given willingly or put together from the times you have chased him down and asked questions he didn't want to answer.

Story 5

The facts: Your school is trying to win a national funding award to help buy loads of new equipment for the science labs. Without winning the award, the school will have to buy the equipment a few pieces at a time and it could take 3 years to collect it all.

The story: This story should cover your school's efforts to win the award and how it would benefit from the new equipment.

Story 6

The facts: Your friend Ronald is desperate to put together a school rock band called the Dozey Flyers. He isn't allowed to practice on site and has nowhere to practice at home either. The teachers are equally desperate to stop Ronald forming the band as he and his band-mates are dreadful – but enthusiastic.

The story: Feature Ronald's struggle for artistic expression. Do you support his bid to make a band? Is he as terrible as the teachers think? Should he be allowed to practice on school property?

Story 7

The facts: It will soon be time for the school play to start. Usually this is organised by Mr Smythe, the drama teacher but as he has been off sick for a few weeks, the Head has asked young Mr Forrest, the music teacher, to take over.

Each year, Mr Smythe has written his own plays, deep and soulful stories of love and loss in the modern world. This year, Mr Forrest has sent away for a full copy of Rats! a musical set in the sewers of New York where the rats sing about freedom and living life in the light.

Mr Smythe has come back early from his sick leave to discover the children already vying for places in Rats! He is furious not to be involved but must take part as he is in charge of acting classes. Mr Forrest is furious that Mr Smythe has come back and keeps interfering in his lovely musical. They keep arguing when they think no one is around.

The story: Here you have the choice to write about the school play in a positive way, downplaying the arguing and concentrating on the play itself. Or you could feature the arguing, which makes a more exciting story but is guaranteed to get you into trouble!

Story 8

The facts: It is time for the children from Jones Primary to descend on school and spend the day. Everyone is ready for them as last year they managed to burn down the P.E. supplies shed and there was also a suspicious incident in the French department.

Whatever happens, Jones Primary must not be allowed to damage the school as this was reported in the local press and your school was criticised for not being able to control a group of 11 year olds.

The story: Decide what happens during the visit and how you will present it. Will you keep it positive, while implying what they might have been up to? Or will you be brutally honest but portray your school as a place of heroes who fought off the barbarian juniors?

3.2 School Times: Write About It!

Task 1: The chosen stories

Look at the available stories and decide which ones you will include and then explain, in detail, why you have chosen them. You should also write about the stories you are forced to include, even though you haven't chosen them yourself. Mention why you think they are being featured (such as, do they make the school look good?).

Explain:

1. Why you have chosen the story

2. What is good about it

3. What might not work so well

4. What the students would like about the story

5. Whether it would be popular with the teachers

6. Would you get into trouble for including the story?

7. What pictures you could feature with each story

Task 2: Your featured stories

Write the stories as they will appear in your newspaper. Include details of any pictures you will feature with them.

Remember, this is for a school newspaper so your language can be informal and chatty. Or you might want to make it sound like a real newspaper and either exaggerate some of the facts or write them as a serious report.

Would you change the tone depending on the story?

3.3 School Times: The Finished Newspaper

Make a mock-up edition of the School Times. Either on the computer or by hand, set out your school newspaper with the stories and pictures included (or marked where the pictures would be).

You should think about how to make it look attractive and eye-catching. You want your new school paper to be popular, especially as you have put so much hard work into finding out exciting news (and uncovering mysteries).

What would your lead story be? And what picture would you have on the front, the first place everyone would look when they picked up your newspaper.

Extra Work

Consider doing two versions of your newspaper, one informal and exciting, with lots of eye-catching headlines and the other more formal and self-important, a serious newspaper covering serious stories.

Think about how these two different approaches would change the style and reading experience. Would you need to completely re-write some of your stories to fit the personality of the newspaper?

3.4 School Times: In Trouble

Scenario

After the publication of your newspaper, you are called to the Head's office. You sit on the Chair of Doom, clutching a copy of the newspaper, wondering why you are here.

Then, just behind the door you hear the Head ranting to the secretary about 'that story' and 'of all stories!' and 'what are we going to do?!'

Which story has landed you in trouble and why?

The door opens and you are called in. Time to explain yourself!

Task 1: Face-to-face

Describe the scene in the Head's office with full details of the reaction to your story and the reason for it. Try to make it a fully rounded scene and not just a description of why you are in trouble.

You should include:

Your own thoughts and feelings

What the Head seems to be thinking and feeling

What is said and how it is expressed

Task 2: I'm Sorry...

You have been forced to offer an apology for the offending story – it's either that or the school newspaper is shut down for good.

Write an apology to be included in the next issue of the school newspaper. Be sincere in your apology but also include a reason why you should not have been punished.

You should think carefully about your **language** in this apology. You need to save the school newspaper but you also want people to know you are not a complete pushover.

For example, you might say something like 'I will try not to offend anyone again', as this implies you are sorry but makes it sound as if you are sorry for offending someone rather than being sorry for publishing the story.

Task 3: What happens next?

Write about the aftermath of your troublesome story and your apology. Is the school newspaper safe? Will you continue to publish controversial news? And does the head have to read every edition before anyone else gets to see it?

4.1 Little Steps Nursery: The Advert

Child Care Supervisor

for award-winning nursery and early learning centre

We have been growing over the last few years and with the completion of our spectacular brand new learning space, we require extra staff to take us into our next successful phase.

Could you be the person we are looking for? Do you have great qualifications and valuable work experience? Do you have the drive and determination it takes to succeed at a job which can be challenging as well as rewarding?

What we need

Level 3 child care qualification

At least 2 years' experience in a related field

Supervision experience

Excellent references

Great customer care skills

Child care assistants

We also need two child care assistants to join our dedicated team. A good knowledge of child care is essential as is a caring and professional manner. Ideally you should have Level 3 in Child Care but we will support the right person as they study for this qualification.

For both jobs, please phone us for a quick chat in the first instance.

4.2 Little Steps Nursery: Looking at the Advert

Look at the jobs advert for Little Steps Nursery.

1. How **effective** is this advert?

Look at details such as text, graphics, font and language used.

2. What is your main impression of Little Steps Nursery from this advert? What kind of place do you think it is?

What language is used to describe the nursery? What effect does this language and the picture used have on your impression of the nursery?

3. Separate fact and opinion within the advert. Are any of the facts based more in opinion or persuasive language?

4. What does the picture add to the advert?

Eg How does it affect the tone? Does it match the advert?

5. Dealing with each job separately, describe the kind of people Little Steps are looking for. You should state your opinions and draw facts from the advert, as well as using the information already given.

Eg Notice how the word caring is used in the assistant job and not the supervisory one.

4.3 Little Steps Nursery: Interview Questions

Scenario

You are the manager of Little Steps Nursery and it is time to hold interviews for the jobs. You have a list of five candidates for the supervisor position and ten for the child care assistants.

You need to fill the vacancies with people who will suit the jobs and also fit in well at the nursery. While it might be more complex to find someone for the supervisor role, you will also want the right person for the assistant role as they have lots of interaction with the children.

When completing the tasks, consider the differences between the job roles and the type of people who would work well in them/

Task 1: Questions and Scenarios

Deal with the jobs separately, while keeping in mind the successful candidates will be working in the same place and alongside each other.

Write down a **list of questions** you will ask the candidates. Make them relevant to the roles involved.

Lots of job interviews include **scenario**s where people have to explain what they would do in different situations.

Think of **one** scenario for each job which would help you to find out what your candidates would do under pressure.

Eg Describe a scenario to them where a child has bumped their head and the candidate needs to explain the injury to the parents. Include extra details such as the parents losing their temper.

Task 2: The Spy

You suspect a rival nursery is sending in a candidate to spy on your business. Think of a way you could find out if one of your candidates isn't quite who they seem to be.

This could be a scenario designed to unsettle them or a question or questions which would draw out the truth or even a situation you create which would reveal the truth.

Consider whether you would be revealing to the candidate (or the rival nursery) that you had discovered their sneaky plans.

4.4 Little Steps Nursery: Interviewers

Scenario

You want to bring in other people to help you with the interviews, with different people to help with each set of interviews. While you will have the final say on who is taken on in the role, you would like other opinions to help you choose your new supervisor and assistants.

Task: The Interviewers

Look at the bios below and choose who would be the best person to help you in the interview. You should choose **two different people**, one for the supervisor interview and one for the assistant interview.

Once you have chosen the people you need, **explain fully** why they are the best choice for each interview. What will they bring to the interview situation? And what difficulties might arise?

Remember, none of your choices are perfect; each will bring positives and negatives to the interview process, depending on their personality and/or their experience.

Bella

Bella is 53 years old and has worked for Little Steps since you opened. She has brought up three children and looked after her ten grandchildren. She is very down-to-earth and can be abrupt when she talks to people, but is very kind to the children. She doesn't like change and is not too keen on expanding the business.

Antony

Antony is your brother. He has invested in the business and needs it to do well but doesn't have much involvement in the day-to-day running of it. He occasionally comes in to supervise the early learning lessons for you as he is a university professor.

Antony is impatient and gets bored easily but is good at working out when people are lying.

Clarissa

Clarissa has only worked for you for a year. She is your best supervisor and can get anything done more quickly than other people. She likes to manage staff more than she likes to work with the children. She can be too organised sometimes and will spend more time making sure the nursery is clean than letting the children play in it.

Clarissa knows exactly what is involved in the supervisor's job and has experience training staff but likes to take over when she can.

Sue

Sue is responsible for dealing with parents at the main reception, sorting out the money, marketing the business and doing the accounts before they are sent to the accountant. Sue likes children and sometimes helps out with child care when you are short staffed. She is a mild person, very quiet and always lets others speak when they need to.

Sue has never supervised staff directly but is often left in charge when you need to pop out. She is very good at dealing with parents.

Daisy

Daisy is your best friend and knows what you want to happen in your business. She has helped set up Little Steps, volunteering to paint and do DIY. She answers the phones if she is nearby and knows all the staff. She isn't officially employed in the nursery but feels a deep connection to it.

Daisy loves to meet new people and chat to them but doesn't always ask the right questions.

4.5 Little Steps Nursery: The Interviews

Scenario

It is time for the interviews for the Supervisor and Assistant roles. You have chosen your questions and your interviewers. You know the type of person you are looking for and also that one of them is a spy from the rival nursery.

Task: Your Candidates

In detail, describe what happens in **four** of the interviews. Write it either as a plain descriptive piece or as a story.

You should write about both job roles but it is up to you whether you split your writing evenly between the interviews or perhaps concentrate on the Supervisor more than the Assistant.

Include:

Details about the candidates

What they are like and what they look like

Your impressions of them

How they present themselves

How well suited they are to the job

Did they impress you?

What did they do wrong

Important!

*Write a full description of their answer to your scenario from **4.3***

Do not include the spy from the rival nursery as you will be writing about this in the next task.

4.6 Little Steps Nursery: The Spy

Scenario

Throughout the interviews you have been looking at the candidates and trying to work out which one is the spy from the rival nursery. You think you know how to work this out but what will you do about it?

Task: Talking to the Spy

Describe the interview with the spy. This should be written in story form and you can include details from the point of view of the spy as well as yourself, if you like.

Include:

How you found out they were the spy

What you think they want to know

How good they are at lying and hiding who they are

What you do about them

Whether they end up reporting back or if you get them on your side

5.1 Tempo Theatre Club: The Poster

Tempo Theatre Club
now also for kids!
Sign up for this fab new
club just for the young
stars of the future!

New
venues
Local
staff

Accredited by
the National
Youth Theatre

Starring
your child!
Coming soon!

Tempo are winners
of the Excellence in
Art Award 2007

Small
classes
Expert
tuition

5.2 Tempo Theatre Club: About the Poster

Scenario

The Tempo Theatre Club is looking for new members. They have run a club for a while but this is the first time they have offered activities for children. They want to make their club sound fun and engaging but at the same time they are very serious about acting and the skills involved.

The members of the club made their own poster as they didn't trust an outside agency to do it properly (also, they don't have much money). As you do the tasks, think about how a 'home-made' poster might be viewed differently than a professional one.

Task 1: The Poster

Look at the poster for the new kid's version of the Tempo Theatre Club. Write a **detailed critique** on the main elements of this poster and how **effective** it is.

Think about the pictures used: how appealing are they? What do they tell you about the club? What do they imply?

Look at the font and layout choices of the text. Does this match the overall approach of the poster?

What type of language is used?

Does it have the right tone to attract clients?

What works and what could be done better?

Task 2: Parents and Children

Imagine you are a parent of a child who would like to join a drama/theatre club. What would attract you in this poster? What would put you off?

Think about how you might react differently to the poster as a parent than if you were a child who was keen to join the club.

5.3 Tempo Theatre Club: More Information

Scenario

It turns out that people want more information about the club so an extra information sheet is created to either email out to people or read from when they telephone. This sheet includes all the details about the club, including prices and times but is still worded to sound attractive and fun.

Task: Persuasive Information

Write the information sheet to go with the poster. This should be a blend of **information** and **persuasive language**.

Include:

When the club will be held and where

How much it will cost and how this can be paid

Details of the instructors involved

Details of general activities within the club as well as the end of season performance

5.4 Tempo Theatre Club: Newspaper Article

Scenario

Interest in the club is building and the local newspaper asks for an article they can run in their entertainments section. They can only give you three paragraphs, unless you pay extra, as then it would be an advertising feature.

Task 1: Short Article

Write a short, three paragraph article for the local newspaper, highlighting the new club and all its attractions. This should include the same information as your information sheet, but the style should be engaging and friendly.

Include:

Concise, relevant information

An attractive headline or phrase to draw people in

Mention the fact this club is a new event for children

Task 2: Advertising Feature

You decide to spend the extra and have an advertising feature. This means you can write a longer article and include extra detail and persuasive language. This longer article gives you more opportunity to sell the club but you still need to include information.

Write the longer article, including all the information from Task 1 and extra phrases and details which would make the club seem more attractive to people.

Consider:

What extra information could you give which is relevant and interesting?

How would your language change in a longer article?

How would you phrase your article to suit it being in a newspaper? Eg could you mention local people being involved?

Would you include pictures now that you have the extra space?

6.1 Leaflets

The Retreat

Relax and explore your inner self in the company of like-minded people. Our adults only retreats are an escape from the pressures of modern life and offer space to think, time to reflect and themed activities to stimulate your innermost soul.

For more information, visit our website www.gofindyerself.com and see how deep within yourself you can dive for the most reasonable monthly sum.

Payment plans available, loans subject to status
All retreats must be paid for in advance

Volunteer!

Robert never saw anyone from one week to the next before Helping Hands stepped in and created an action plan to bring him help, support and a feeling of friendship in his life. Now he is looking forward to the future and knows Help is just a phone call away. To make a difference to someone like Robert, get in touch at the number below and see how anyone can change the life of someone in need, just by reaching out to them.

Looking to volunteer?

Find out how you can make a difference in your local community

Helping Hands is now working in your community to change the lives of the elderly and in need

Fully funded by public donations

Call 01853 22357 and start to help today! Volunteers always welcome!

The Shop

Nana's Little Darlings

Children's boutique fashions

Gloriously good quality and timeless designs

Come to our grand opening and find out why luxury is is not just for grown ups!

6.2 Leaflets: A Closer Look

Scenario

These three leaflets have been created for very different purposes. One is for a (paid for) retreat, another wants to recruit volunteers and the third is advertising an exclusive childrenswear shop.

Task: In Detail

Look at the three leaflets and answer the following questions about **each of them**:

1. Who is the target audience?

Think about age and type of person, family situation, financial standing.

2. Is the leaflet about the target audience or is it about another group of people?

Eg the Helping Hands leaflet is aimed at volunteers but is about helping the elderly.

3. Would the leaflet be attractive to its target audience? Why or why not?

Examine whether the language used and presentation is attractive to the intended audience. Does it make them want to know more or put them off?

4. Describe the language used and the overall tone of the leaflet. Give

examples to support your answer.

Is the language suitable to the audience? Does it persuade the reader or patronise them?

5. How effective is the leaflet?

Think about what the leaflet wants to do and decide if it succeeds. For instance, the Helping Hands leaflet wants to attract volunteers – does it portray this well enough? What could be done more effectively?

6.3 Leaflets: Improving on the Original

Scenario

These leaflets all have faults as well as elements which attract their target audience. Think about how improvements would make the leaflets more successful and either create an audience for their product or benefit the community, such as in the volunteering leaflet.

Task 1: Changes

Again working through the leaflets, what would you change about each leaflet to make it more effective? For instance, do you need to change the whole leaflet to make it better or just alter certain parts, such as the wording or the picture?

Task 2: New Versions

Now design your own version of each leaflet, either changing it completely or altering it to make it better.

This is your chance to do it differently and improve on the original. You can change anything and everything, as long as you keep the main information, such as the name of the company or the most important details, such as what is offered.

7.1 The Community Club: The Report

Scenario

You have been asked to organise a new club at your local community centre. The club is for retired people who want to meet during the day for a chat and to learn new skills. The emphasis is on making a friendly club which will also introduce people to new experiences and skills.

Task: Reporting

Write a **report**, including all the important details about the club as well as how you plan to organise setting it up. Your language should be quite **formal** and **descriptive**. If there are any details you are unsure of (such as how the club will be funded) then be honest when describing this – your report does not need to have all the answers.

Decide what **new skills** members might learn (either something ongoing or a selection of different ones).

Include the following details:

How often will the club meet? How long will the sessions be?

Will it be free/how much will it cost?

If free, how might the club be funded?

Would you run the club with volunteers or paid staff?

Would any extras be included eg refreshments or supplies for activities?

Does any equipment need to be purchased?

Will local businesses be asked to sponsor the club?

What methods will you use to advertise and attract members?

4. Encourage would-be volunteers to help run the club or teach new skills.

7.2 The Community Club: The Flyer

Scenario

Now you need to let people know about the new community club. You decide to put out a flyer: this is like an informational poster, not as detailed as a leaflet but more than just a normal advert.

Your flyer will be A4 size and needs to include enough information to attract people without filling up too much space with words. You should balance out the information with attractive images of what will happen at the club.

Task: Design a Flyer

Create a flyer for your new club. Do this in stages:

1. Decide what **information** you need to include on the flyer.

2. What **images** would work best (images supporting the information as well as attracting potential members).

3. **Design** your flyer so that words and images are arranged in the most effective and attractive layout.

You should consider:

The language used – a mixture of descriptive and persuasive

How will you make it attractive to the older people who might join your club?

How much information do they need? And what kind of information will make them want to find out more?

What colour scheme do you think would be appealing to your target audience?

What will you use as your title or main headline?

How do you think they will want to contact you?

Do you also want to appeal to anyone who might want to help out at the club?

7.3 The Community Club: Looking at your Flyer

Scenario

Now you are going to look again at your flyer, treating it as if you have never seen it before. Try to distance yourself from it and examine it anew. If you think this may be difficult, leave this exercise for a few days and come back to it. You can also try asking someone else what they think of your flyer and take some ideas from their responses to get you started.

Task: Critique Yourself

Answer the following questions, being careful to **critique your own work** – don't be kind to yourself!

1. How does the flyer engage the reader?

Include information on graphics, layout, headers, etc as well as persuading text.

2. How can people find out more information about the club? Is the target audience catered for? (eg would retired people rather telephone for information or would they email?)

3. Why do the activities in the flyer appeal to the target audience?

4. How successful do you think the flyer might be and why?

5. Is there anything which could have been done better?

7.4 The Community Club: The Website

Scenario

The club is gathering momentum and you want to support your flyer with a simple, but informative, website where people can find out more, see plans of the community centre and get in touch with you if they prefer emails to telephone calls.

The website gives you the chance to add any details which were left out of the flyer and also to add lots of images of the community centre. This way, people can see where the club will be held without having to wait until the first meeting. You can also include information about anyone who is helping with the club.

Task: The Home Page

Using your own **flyer** and the information from your **report**, design and write the home page of the club website.

Think about any changes you might make for a website rather than a flyer and how focussed you would be on the community aspect of your club.

Consider:

How much information would you include

What type of images you might use

How would you link up the leaflet and the website?

Think about colour schemes, font, layout

How would your use of language change compared to writing a flyer or a report?

7.5 The Community Club: Newsletter

Scenario

You have had four meetings already, managing to attract fifteen people to your new club. Some of them are very keen but a few say they might not come back next time. You have set up different activities and some are more popular than others. You are determined to make the club a success and know it can work.

Task: Persuasive News

Write a **newsletter** to send out to local people. This is your chance to give detailed information to possible new members, so make it sound attractive and interesting. Keep your language **informal** but with plenty of **facts**.

Follow the points below to write up your newsletter but feel free to add anything extra that you think will make it work.

1. Give specific facts about the meetings, such as how many people turned up and what they did.

2. Describe anything that might bring the clubs to life. eg if you ran a pottery class, perhaps you could include a funny story about the clay flying off across the room.

3. Make sure it sounds as if everyone is making friends.

4. Think of a problem you have encountered and describe how it was resolved in a positive way.

5. Include information on how to join but make this seem part of the main text rather than a mini-advert for the club.

6. You have space for only 2 pictures. What might you include in the newsletter, to back up everything you have said?

7.6 The Community Club: Reggie's Letter

Scenario

Reggie has been to the club every single week, mainly because his lady friend Maisie also attends. He is very keen to help you make the club popular but he is also a bit bossy and likes to think he helps you to run it when actually he gets in the way.

Task: Reggie's Words

Reggie writes a letter to the local paper to promote the club. Write this letter for Reggie, putting his bossy tone into the language you use. Think about what someone like Reggie might include.

Consider:

What does he think is important in the club?

What activities might he suggest for the club?

How would he make it sound as if he was running the club?

Would his letter attract people or put them off?

7.7 The Community Club: A Speech

Scenario

You have been asked to come and speak about your new club. Your audience is a mixture of ages but will include plenty of people who might be interested in joining. There will also be people listening who could help at the club, bringing a great variety of skills to attract new members and keep people coming back.

Task: Speaking to Persuade

Write a speech which will give people information and make them want to find out more and maybe join the club. Include an invitation to anyone who might want to volunteer but try to make it a natural part of your speech.

Include the following points and anything else you think would attract new members and helpers:

1. Keep it clear and **easy to understand**: if people want to pass on information to others, they need to know the important points.

2. Describe a **typical club meeting**, including the social side and the activity.

3. Talk about **how you started the club** and what you meant it to be like at the beginning.

4. Mention **how it has changed** over time.

5. Include a **difficulty** you have overcome.

6. Include **a few quotes** from club members.

8.1 Descriptions: Known vs Unknown

Scenario

In this section you will be looking at how differently your writing develops if you are describing the familiar or unfamiliar. This can include places you know well or somewhere you have only been once or twice, as well as people you could describe easily compared to strangers you meet for the first time.

You should consider how your deeper knowledge of a place, person or situation changes the way you write about it. If you are familiar with something you will probably include different details because you don't have to think about the subject as much.

Task 1: Known

Describe a place which is very familiar to you, such as a room in your house or a place at school. Make sure it is somewhere you know well enough to describe without any difficulty. It should be a place you can visualise when you close your eyes.

Now, while you are visualising the familiar place, write a full description of it. This should include the big, obvious things like furniture or the colour scheme, as well as smaller, less noticeable details like the pattern on the carpet, the fabric of the curtains, how big the light bulbs are.

What you are looking to do is create a **detailed descriptive piece** which includes elements of the room you normally would either take for granted or have not properly noticed. It doesn't matter if your finished piece is not exciting! The main aim is to practice your descriptive technique.

Read my example and notice how I have included different elements of description. I have chosen the inside of my car, a place which is the same for lots of people. To make it my own, I have included details which specifically describe my own car, such as going to the beach.

Try to include these layers of description in your own writing, so that what seems like a place lots of people could describe becomes your own and personal to the way you use it.

Example Known

The car is quite small inside. The body is black and the upholstery is an old-fashioned grey pattern, with squares all over it. There are mats on the floor which have moved so that they don't protect it as much as they did. There is also sand on the floor, from trips to the beach.

In the middle of the car, above the car radio and vents, is a little space for Important Stuff. I keep my sunglasses there, in a Hello Kitty case, a hair brush and some tissues. There is also an elastic band.

In the side of the door is a space for more Important Stuff. I have a time-

disc for parking and a packet of Christmas cards. I will take these out
before Easter.

Behind the driver's seat is a blue umbrella with frills and a hooked handle.
It lies across the space, waiting for the next deluge. Today my coat lies on
top of it, bright pink against blue.

Task: Unknown

Now describe somewhere more **unfamiliar**. Although I have used the title
Unknown here, it doesn't have to be a place which is completely strange to
you. What you need is somewhere that you could not describe very easily
without being there. A good example might be the house of a friend or
relative where you have a vague idea of how things look but couldn't sit
down and write a detailed description. Otherwise, choose somewhere
completely new and try describing it.

The Unknown description can be very similar to the Known description:
write down every detail, working through them carefully to give the fullest
piece of writing. Imagine you are walking into the Unknown place for the
first time (you may even be doing that). What do you notice? What jumps
out at you and what would you not see until later?

Example Unknown

My example is the local college foyer. It is somewhere I have been a
handful of times. Notice how the details of a place like this are different
from my description of the inside of my car.

The foyer has confusing glass sliding doors, with big buttons I press to make them open. It's hard to see where the door ends and the wall begins. Once through, I find myself in an open space, with a reception desk way off to one side. To reach the desk I have to weave my way through groups of students, all of whom know where they are going.

At the reception desk I see there is another set of offices, with more glass walls, set off to the side. It is like this area is part of the college and the rest is just a space to fill with students. This area seems quieter and more welcoming, with little sofas tucked in a corner and along a wall and pot plants on the reception desk and on the desks inside the other office.

I am given a badge to open the doors to the rest of college and away I go, across the foyer, gently fighting my way through the melee of students and hoping no one stands on me.

Do you see how this description is less straightforward than the one of my car? I include more personal details, such as when I have to fight to get past the students. The description also changes because I am describing a much larger space.

This description is less about a blow-by-blow account of the place and more about how I see it when I go in. I have described it in a more personal way, to show that this is a first impression.

8.2 Descriptions: Stranger vs Friend

Scenario

For this exercise, I want you to look at the way you describe **people**. We are talking about real people and not characters in books or stories. If you are describing a **person you know**, then you will include different details than if you are trying to describe a complete **stranger**. It is likely that you would describe the person you know using more emotive words which explain what kind of personality they have, whereas when you describe a stranger you might talk more about how they look and what they appear to be.

Task: Stranger

Firstly, I want you to describe a stranger. Choose one of the pictures below and imagine you are standing in front of the real person, with enough time to look at them and note any important features. You will also want to think about what kind of job they might do or even their personality, based solely on your **first impressions**.

What assumptions did you make about the people and their personalities or activities? Did you base any personality points on how they looked or what they were doing?

Task: Friend

Now describe someone you know well. They don't actually have to be a friend but you should be very familiar with the way they look and know a good amount about their personalities.

Include what the person looks like and wears, but also say what type of personality they have, what they like doing and so on. Make it more about the whole person than a first impression. And be honest in what you say as they won't see this unless you show them!

9.1 Feelings: The Beginning

Describing feelings can be a tricky business. You may have a sense of how you want to explain them and then be faced with looking for ten different ways to describe sadness or irritation.

For this exercise, we are using the parts of a story so that you can see how feelings can be worked into your writing as a story progresses.

Scenario

You are going to stay with your big sister, Catherine, at her new holiday home by the sea. She is sharing it with her best friend Abigail, who used to bother you a lot at school and would have bullied you if Catherine hadn't been there.

The Beginning

You are seeing Abigail for the first time since school and she seems much nicer than she was back then. Perhaps she has grown up at last? But no, on your first day at the holiday home she reveals herself to still be as spiteful and sneaky as ever.

Task

Write a story section about this first day with Abigail. Include how you feel seeing her again. Don't jump right into not trusting her, make it gradual and imagine how you would feel in that situation.

This is the beginning of your feelings and you should treat it as an introduction, a build-up to what comes in later.

Don't forget, there is no need to just describe feelings, you can imply them or let the reader imagine how you feel. For instance, instead of saying you are uncomfortable, you could describe a situation where Abigail 'accidentally' spills her drink on you and pretends to be sorry, while secretly laughing. You wouldn't need to fully describe feeling upset and annoyed for the reader to imagine you felt this way.

Look at my example beginning to see how you can start your story with only a hint of what is to come.

Example Beginning

Dragging my suitcase up the little path to the holiday home, I looked at Catherine and smiled. My smile wavered as Abigail appeared behind her, grinning and making a goofy thumbs-up signal, as if she had done something clever.

I managed a proper smile at her, determined not to let the past spoil our holiday. Then, just for a second, I thought I saw her face change to the old smug, superior expression. I blinked. No, she was smiling, that was all. I mustn't let my mind play tricks on me.

9.2 Feelings: The Middle

Scenario

Now we are in the thick of it. Abigail has revealed herself to be even worse than when she was at school and your sister Catherine still thinks she is a great person. You know from experience that it's no good trying to talk to Catherine about it, you will just have to deal with Abigail yourself – after all, it's your holiday too!

Task

Write another story section, this time starting right after Abigail has done something nasty. Your section should start while you are in the grip of strong emotions, whether these are anger, sorrow, fear or righteous fury! You can describe what Abigail has done or concentrate on your feelings without explaining the event. Don't forget, you are not writing the full story so you can leave some things to the imagination.

Look at my example to see how you might begin then write your own story section.

Example Middle

I stood, unable to move I was so shocked. How could she? What was she thinking? But even as I started to shake the oil from my hands, I knew how she could and what she was thinking: she had always enjoyed upsetting me and she was just being her usual self. Only now, all these years later, she was still behaving like a stupid, nasty, vindictive little madam. Well, one of us had grown up and it was obviously not her!

Just you wait, Abigail, I thought. This time, things are going to be different.

9.3 Feelings: The End

Scenario

Finally, the holiday is coming to an end. Abigail has revealed herself to be even worse than when she was at school because now she is a grown woman with her own job who should know better. And she still sees you as a source of entertainment!

Task

This section does not have to be the very end of the story but it should be close to it. You should wrap up the drama with Abigail, one way or the other. This can mean walking away without trying to make her pay, ignoring her and enjoying the rest of the holiday, having it out with Abigail to make her stop, taking revenge or anything else you think would make a good ending.

Still focus on your feelings but also include a small event which shows how things have turned out in the end. In my example, look at where I mention the coffee cup to see the small event which shows Abigail is not as tough as she thinks she is.

If you are not sure how to end the story, try working with different emotions and see how scenes play out. What you write the first time does not have to be your final effort.

Example End

I watched as the tiny, fragile, beautiful cup spun off the table and onto the floor. It hit the tiles and smashed, magically changing from an antique keepsake to a sad little mess. Abigail watched it fall, knowing it was her fault and she would never have it back. Her grandmother's tea cup, broken because Abigail couldn't keep her temper.

Her face crumpled and she fought back the tears, one hand raised as if she could stop herself crying and the other hand reaching feebly towards the cup.

10.1 Personality Switch: Introduction

For this section, we are going to work with one character, **Jilly**.

Jilly is 16 years old and has just finished taking her exams. These exercises are set in the summer after she leaves school.

We will look at her personality and how her own behaviour – and that of other people – is affected by her personality type. Then we will see how a change in personality affects what we might write about Jilly and her life.

When you write about a character, it's very important to show their personality. Sometimes you can do this by **direct description**:

Jilly was always offending people.

You can also show it by **what happens in the story**:

Jilly laughed her head off when she saw Sam's new hairstyle. She didn't stop until Sam started to cry.

You can also show a character's personality by **how they speak** in their own dialogue:

'Why are you upset?' Jilly asked, pulling a face. 'If you want to do that to your hair then it's your own fault if people laugh. Grow up!'

These different ways each show us that Jilly offends people, but some are more effective than others. In the direct description, it isn't really enough to say that Jilly offends people; you need more detail to realise that she is not just offensive but quite unkind with it.

You should really avoid long descriptions on their own though – it is always better to show what a person is like, through their behaviour or dialogue, than to simply describe it for the reader.

So, what do the excerpts above tell us about Jilly?

She offends people.

She does not mind offending people.

She is possibly unkind as most people wouldn't laugh until the other person cried.

She doesn't blame herself for being unkind, she actually blames the other person for having a hairstyle she finds funny.

She is disrespectful.

10.2 Personality Switch: Character bio

Scenario

We have some basic facts about Jilly, such as her age, her situation and some elements of her personality. How much do we really know about her though?

If you write about a character, even if you don't include lots of details, it helps to feel you know them as well as possible. For instance, you might only need to write a short story about someone but if you have worked out who they are and what they are like, it becomes much easier to make them sound like a real person in your story.

Task: Who is Jilly?

Write a character bio for Jilly. Work out the aspects of her personality, based on what I have already said. Decide if you want to include anything else which might be important, especially if this helps to make her feel like a fully rounded person. For instance, you might decide she often upsets people but also has a softer side, or you might make her out to be a completely unlikeable character.

Feel free to add extra details to the bio which you wouldn't necessarily add to your writing later.

You might want to include:

What she looks like

What music she likes

Did she enjoy school? Why or why not?

How well does she get on with her family?

Does she have any pets?

What does she do in her spare time?

10.3 Personality Switch: Jilly's Mistake

Scenario

Jilly works part-time at an office. Her job is to organise the invoices from customers and send out reminders for payment. She likes the computer work and talking to the other people in the office but she sometimes forgets to send out the first reminders on late invoices. This means the company gets paid later than they should.

This time, Jilly has made it even worse. She not only forgot to send out the payment reminder, she then forgot she hadn't sent it and posted the follow-up reminder, which only gives customers a week to pay their full bill.

The customer has called the company and is complaining *a lot*. Jilly's boss wants a word with her about it…

Task: Facing the Boss

Write about what happens when Jilly has to explain herself to her boss. Include:

Descriptions of how Jilly and her boss behave

Dialogue

How Jilly gets out of trouble

Look at my example for ideas on how to mix events in a story while showing the personality of your character/s.

Example

Jilly walked into the boss's office with a smile on her face. She had decided to play dumb and pretend someone else made the mistake. After all, they couldn't prove it was her and she needed this job.

The manager looked at her and sighed, staring back down at his desk. Jilly's stomach lurched; was he going to sack her anyway? Maybe she should be honest for once?

Quick re-think, she decided as she took longer than necessary to sit down. Play dumb still but then, when she was in trouble, cry a bit and look lost. He couldn't sack her if she looked lost, could he? It always worked when she was in trouble at school.

10.4 Personality Switch: Jilly's Birthday

Scenario

It is Jilly's birthday and, despite being awkward with people most of the year, she does love being the centre of attention on her special day. She always has a party and she invites people who will definitely come, as well as some who would rather do anything else *but* come.

Task 1: Jilly's Point of View

Using what you know about Jilly's personality, write about her birthday. You can decide what she does, who she sees and how she behaves.

Include:

An argument

A happy moment

A new friend

Task 2: A Different Point of View

Choose part of what you have already written about Jilly's birthday and create a **new scene** from it. This time you are going to write from the point of view of another person involved.

It can be a very short scene taken from the original, or the whole piece re-written. Don't worry if you need to change or rearrange something to make it work; the most important element of this section is writing from a **different perspective**.

Include:

A description of Jilly, either how she looks, behaves, or her personality

How the person feels about her and why

Their opinion of the birthday party

10.5 Personality Switch: Back in the Office

Scenario

Now Jilly is going to have a **personality makeover**. Using the office scenario with Jilly's boss, think about how this might have turned out if Jilly had a **different personality**.

Remember, she is still making mistakes and causing problems at work, so even if you decide she is now a nicer person, would this get her out of trouble? How would her new personality change the situation?

Task: All change

Switch Jilly's personality for one of the types described below. Once you have decided on her new personality, think about how this would affect the outcome of her situation.

Use your original scenario to work out what might happen. Look at my example to see how you can change things around. I have used the personality type 'scared of her own shadow'.

Personality types

Shrewd and aware of other people

Careful of what she says and does

Scared of her own shadow

Finds everything funny

Likes taking risks

Kind and likes to stay calm

Loves talking about people

Example

Jilly walked into the boss's office with a fearful smile on her face, trying not to look as terrified as she felt. She had decided to admit it was all her fault and ask for more training, in the hopes she wouldn't be fired. She really needed this job.

The manager looked at her and sighed, staring back down at his desk. Jilly's stomach lurched; was he going to sack her anyway? Maybe she should just run out in case he started shouting at her?

10.6 Personality Switch: Another Birthday

Scenario

Now you are going to re-write Jilly's birthday, still from her point of view and with a **new personality**. This is not about treating Jilly as if she is a whole new person; think of how original events might change if she behaved differently.

Task: Still Arguing?

Read your original birthday scenario and work out how it might change if you choose a different personality type. Using the list from the previous exercise, choose **another new personality** and re-write your scenario.

This time, focus on the **argument** part of the scenario. If you need to, create some extra details so that you can write more about the argument than you did originally. Otherwise, change the way the argument plays out to reflect the new personality.

Look at my examples below. I have written the start of two arguments, one with Jilly's original personality and one using the new personality type of 'finds everything funny'. Notice how I keep the main details the same but change how Jilly behaves (which, in turn, would probably change how the other person behaved too).

Example Argument 1

Jilly narrowed her eyes and marched up to Sasha. She jabbed at the girl's shoulder and said,

'So, you think you can just walk in and tell my friends what to do? Who do you think you are?'

Sasha jumped round to look at Jilly, rubbing her arm where she had been jabbed.

'I don't think I can tell anybody anything!' she hissed back. 'You're just not used to people standing up to you.'

Example Argument 2

Jilly rolled her eyes and rushed up to Sasha, nipping her on the opposite shoulder so she looked the wrong way to see who was there.

'You'll have to be quicker than that!' Jilly said, laughing as Sasha glared at her. 'And you shouldn't be telling my friends what to do, either. If they want to be my friends, that's none of your business.'

She sniggered as Sasha looked even angrier. There was nothing funnier than annoying people who took things too seriously.

10.7 Personality Switch: What Next?

Scenario

Now you are free to create an original situation for Jilly, complete with her old and new personalities. Think about her life as you know it and the things she might do. What event or situation do you think might work well?

Task: What's New?

Choose a new situation for Jilly and write a short story or story segment for her. Everything that happens within it is up to you but you will be changing Jilly's personality within the story.

Split the story into **three parts**. They should follow on naturally from one to the other but each part should give Jilly a different personality. So she might start by being Jilly the bully, then change to being timid and end with laughing at everything.

Try writing a **detailed plan** so that you are sure what will happen when. This can make it easier to change Jilly's personality as you will not be worrying about events as well as Jilly herself.

Look at my short example to see how this might look.

Example Story

Bully: *Jilly bulldozed her way through the crowd of small children, only thinking about getting to the front where the Punch and Judy van stood.*

Timid: *She stopped when she reached the van, unsure what she should do now she was here. Jilly was sure the Punch and Judy man had stolen her bracelet but how could she prove it?*

Funny: *Jilly decided to make fun of him til he came out - it would be fun and it might work. She yelled with the kids, taunting him and hooting with laughter every time he got something wrong. By the end of the act, the little Punch puppet was shaking with rage.*

11.1 The Hostel: Introduction

This section is based around a school trip to a hostel and you should complete all the exercises in **diary format**. So you should write in the first person, describing events as if you were really there. You can change who *you* are though, so feel free to become a different personality if you think it will help you tell the story.

When using a diary format to tell a story, it is really important to remember that you are re-telling events which have already happened. Unlike normal stories in the first person, you are in a position to **write about events**, which means you have escaped any danger or difficulty and made it back to your diary. This has an effect on any **suspense** you try to build as your reader knows you have survived, so you need to think how you can build suspense even though you are writing after the events.

One way to do this is to have your diary with you at all times. For instance, in one of the exercises you are writing while hiding from danger, so although you are fine at that moment, danger is imminent and you are not safe. This is a way to combine suspense and the diary format.

Another way is to leave the reader unsure of how safe other people are in your story. You might be writing about what happened but if you make it suspenseful and include other people in the story, then your reader wants to know what happens to the others.

Although this introduction is based around building suspense, your exercises in this section do not have to be all about danger and fear. You can have a funny story which still makes your reader keen to find out more, or you can have an adventure story which includes comedy, fear, drama etc, without simply re-telling the story. **Intrigue and mystery** should be built into your story-telling in this section, but the rest is up to you.

11.2 The Hostel: Assembly

Scenario

Every year your school sends students away to stay in France or Austria on a lovely, but expensive, holiday. This year there is not enough money for the usual trip so students are going on an action-packed adventure holiday in a hostel in the North of England. The brochure looks like it was printed years ago and the hostel building looks a bit run-down and rickety in the pictures.

You don't want to go on an action-packed holiday and would much rather stay at home but you have been volunteered by your favourite teacher to help with the whole trip. Feeling like you have no choice but to help out, you find yourself agreeing to talk to a whole school assembly...

Task: Sign Them Up!

Your teacher wants you to persuade people in school to come on the trip by giving a talk in assembly. You need to make the hostel holiday sound **exciting** and **different**.

In your diary, write about your talk to the assembly and how it all worked out. You need to include:

Some of the persuasive language you used in your speech

Some details of the trip

How you felt giving the talk

How people reacted to what you had to say

An example of the questions you were asked

How many people signed up for the trip

A description of what the hostel looks like in the brochure (run down and rickety) compared to how you described it in the assembly (how would you use positive description?)

Important!

For this task you not only need to think about your diary entry, but the talk you gave to the assembly. Try writing some notes on your talk, or even the full speech. This will help you to turn the imaginary talk into a diary entry written after the event.

11.3 The Hostel: The Journey

Scenario

You finally set off for the hostel; you, your teachers and other pupils all cooped up in an old bus with no toilet. The roads seem to get smaller and smaller as the bus rumbles further away from home and school.

Eventually, the bus finds the bumpy path to the hostel. It is the only building for miles around and you can't see it until the bus turns the final corner.

The hostel building, which already looked quite bad in the pictures, looks far worse in real life. The walls are covered in ivy, the window frames are rotting, the front door has a hole where the letter box should be and, as the bus pulls up, a pigeon flies out of a hole in the roof.

Task: Getting There

Write in your diary as if you are describing the journey up to the point where the pigeon flies out of the roof. You have time to finish your entry because your teacher leaves you all on the bus while he goes to see if this is really the right place.

You should describe how you **feel** about the journey and include at least **three** of the following:

What it was like travelling in the bus

Who was ill

Who caused trouble

How long the journey took

Were you allowed to listen to music and play games?

Which teachers came with you and what they are like

11.4 The Hostel: First Night

Scenario

You are shown to your rooms by the only person who seems to be around when you arrive, **Jed Cargill**. He is in his twenties but looks older. He has straggly hair and dirty clothes and keeps scratching under his armpits when he talks to people.

The rooms are quite big and cleaner than the rest of the place but the beds are very old and creaky. The sheets are cold, as if no one has slept here for a very long time. Each room has bunk beds and can sleep four people.

The walls in the hostel are cold concrete, undecorated and there is no central heating. There is one very big fireplace in the main hall but Jed says the wood is too wet to light. The only modern room in the whole place is the kitchen.

Task 1: Settling In

It is your first night in the hostel and you are settling down for sleep. You and your school mates are trying to make the best of things, getting used to the chilly rooms and unwelcoming beds.

Write about how you are feeling as you settle down for the night.

You should include:

Who you are sharing the room with

What you and other people think of the place

What you think of Jed

Your impressions of what your time away will be like

Task 2: What Was That Noise?

At some stage in the night you are woken up by a strange noise. It is still fully dark outside as you lie in your bed, waiting to see if the noise comes again.

Write about what happens when you are woken up.

You should include:

Being woken by a mysterious noise

How you feel about waking in the cold, dark, unfamiliar place

Whether you get up to investigate

A strange feeling that comes over you when you hear another noise, right outside your window

11.5 The Hostel: A New Day

Scenario

Your first proper day at the hostel and you all wake up, expecting the action-packed holiday to begin. When you come to breakfast, you discover Jed is still the only person around and your teachers are looking increasingly anxious. Jed says more helpers will turn up soon and dishes out hot, sweet porridge to the whole group.

Jed is almost like a different person today, full of chatter and much friendlier than he was the day before. Also, he has stopped scratching his armpits and looks a lot cleaner.

He says the first activity is to learn housekeeping skills and he sends you all out to find firewood and chop logs. After that, he says you can go down to the field and look for wild mushrooms.

You put up with this for a while but then decide this is not the holiday you signed up for. You persuaded people to come here and you want to help them have a good time. When no one is looking, you sneak off to explore.

Task: How Did I Get Here?

It is three hours since you sneaked away and no one knows where you are. You are hiding in a shed with only your diary for company.

Describe what has happened to you in as much detail as possible, deciding whether you will present it as exciting, mysterious, scary, strange or inexplicable.

You should include:

How you feel

How you came to be in the shed

If there is any chance of people finding out where you are

How you plan to get out

11.6 The Hostel: The Truth

Scenario

It turns out the hostel has not been open for visitors for many years. The brochure sent to the school is more than ten years old. And Jed is not who he appears to be…

Now you are going to try and tell everyone the truth about the hostel, whether they want to believe you or not.

The tasks are split between telling everyone the truth and the very end of the same day.

Task 1: What's Going On?

You are going to tell everyone the truth and then write about it afterwards, in your diary. You can decide what the truth is but once you have revealed it, people become angry and you disappear to your room for a while – which is where you are writing in your diary.

Work out what is happening at the hostel, including the likely outcome of revealing the truth. Will it be dangerous? Or will it all be based in a normal, everyday situation?

You should include:

What is really happening at the hostel?

Who is Jed?

How you plan to reveal the truth

What you expect to happen afterwards

Task 2: The End of the Day

This final diary entry is written after everything has come to an end. It is a few hours since you were sitting in your room after you told everyone the truth. What has happened since then?

You should include:

What happened after you had been in your room

What became of Jed

How you feel about your whole experience at the hostel

What happened in the end?

12.1 What Am I Thinking?
Description

Introduction

This is a **descriptive** exercise where you will use an image of a person to build up an idea of what they are **thinking**. You will work with one picture at a time, following the points set out below in the **Task** section as well as one piece of **extra information** underneath each picture.

The questions in the **Task** section are general and apply to all the pictures. The **extra information** helps you to set the scene and bring some real-life depth to your writing.

Don't be afraid to make up details to fit the picture. The most important thing is to explain and describe what the person is thinking about. Any details you add should back up your description, even if you have no idea if they are true.

I have included a fully completed example to help you.

Task

For each of the images below, take notice of the **extra information** and also describe the following:

1. What is the person thinking about?

2. What does the expression reveal about the person's thoughts?

3. What type of person do you think they are?

Example

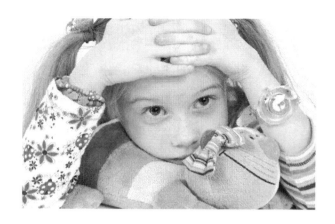

It is very late at night

What is the person thinking about? *I think the little girl has seen someone arguing and wants to hide from it. She is watching something going on, at the same time as wanting to hide.*

What does the expression reveal about the person's thoughts? *The little girl has a wary and tired expression. She looks as if she wants to hide from something but cannot. She is snuggled into her toy as if she is hiding behind it and using it for comfort.*

What type of person do you think she is? *She looks quiet and thoughtful. She is probably braver than she is feeling because she is taking comfort* *from her toy instead of running away.*

Notice how my example uses the picture but I make my own conclusions about what is going on. I don't know if the little girl has seen an argument, I am just drawing out my own extra details from the way she looks in the photograph.

Picture One

The clock has just chimed nine

Picture Two

I'm not going back to school!

Picture Three

The room should have been empty

Picture Four

I wonder if it's true?

Picture Five

The perfect present – me!

Picture Six

And then the door opened

Picture Seven

I've no idea what went wrong

12.2 What Am I Thinking? Story

Scenario

I now want you to look at your pictures and descriptions as if they were a **story**.

You may already have phrased your answers as if they are a story. If so, then expand on your work and delve more into the picture. If you have written normal descriptions for each picture, then think about how you would change those to become a story.

Don't worry, I am not expecting you to write about all the pictures again! You only need to work with two of the pictures but include more if you want to extend this section.

I have included a full example, based on my example in the last task. Use this to help you re-write your own descriptions as a story.

Task

Choose **two** of the pictures from the first part of this section. Try to choose pictures or descriptions which are very different from each other, either in mood or the way you have described them.

Now imagine you are seeing the events behind the picture, as well as the person you have already described. Write about them and their feelings and situation in the form of a story.

Use my example to help you. I have included the original example again so you can compare it easily with the finished story.

Example

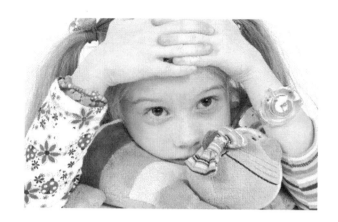

It is very late at night

What is the person thinking about? *I think the little girl has seen someone arguing and wants to hide from it. She is watching something going on, at the same time as wanting to hide.*

What does the expression reveal about the person's thoughts? *The little girl has a wary and tired expression. She looks as if she wants to hide from something but cannot. She is snuggled into her toy as if she is hiding behind it and using it for comfort.*

What type of personality do you think the person has? *She looks quiet and thoughtful. She is probably braver than she is feeling because she is taking comfort from her toy instead of running away.*

Example Story

Jessie came out onto the landing and looked down into the hall where her parents stood staring at each other, their faces pale. For a moment there was silence, then they started shouting again, throwing insults and taking no notice of the little girl at the top of the stairs.

Did they see her? Did they care? Jessie sat down, then lay down, burrowing her face into Toggle. At least he loved her.

Jessie waited so long that her fear turned into exhaustion and as the argument simmered down to nothing, she fell asleep, her face still resting on Toggle's soft back. That was how her parents found her when they finally came up to bed.

13.1 Writing in Stages: Introduction

This section is about **writing in stages**, fulfilling each part of the task without knowing exactly what lies ahead. You start with an idea which is quite vague and gives you plenty of opportunity to make up your own story. Once you have written the beginning of the story, you move on to the middle which will be a change in direction.

At this point you need to work on incorporating what you have already written with the new idea. Stories often change as they progress but you might have to combine your own beginning with an idea that seems to have nothing to do with your starting point.

Once you have finished the middle you complete the story by moving in another new direction. You should try to make sure your story reads well and not as though it's held together with paper clips!

The **three sections** will work like this:

*Beginnings are vague and **fluid**, based on a broad idea*

*Middles have a specific **event** you need to work into your story*

*Endings bring in a particular **feeling**, as described in one word or phrase*

There will be plenty of opportunity to write what you like; the main challenge in this exercise is making the story work as **one piece of writing**, as well as including the specific event in the middle.

You can create any characters and events you like and follow a certain theme, such as horror, comedy etc.

Important!

Do not peek ahead to the next section! Look at the Beginnings and work from those, *then* move on to the Middles to see which specific event you need to include. Do not progress from one part of the story to another before you have finished writing about it. You should be completely unaware of your choices before you see them.

Feel free to use ideas from the pictures between the sections but they are really there to stop you peeking!

A re-write?

If you would like to repeat this exercise using different choices for your sections, then obviously you will know what you have to choose from the second or third time around. If you decide to try again, think about how you can work towards a particular ending. By choosing the ending first, you bring in some extra difficulty with the rest of your story which should make up for knowing which choices are ahead.

13.2 Writing in Stages: Beginnings

Choose one of the beginnings listed below. Don't be afraid to include lots of detail in your writing – just because you will be given a specific event in the next section does not mean you should try to keep this section open and vague.

Look at my examples in each section to help you form your story.

Beginnings

A white, swirling mist

Suddenly it was there

Often, it felt cold

Rocks tumbling

'I have no idea!' she laughed

The car door slammed

The garden was a wilderness

Toby shrugged

The seagull screamed

Quickly, they reached

Example Beginning

(For this example, I have used the *Quickly, they reached* beginning).

Sonny looked round to see his friends scrambling over the rocks behind him. Little Lou was having trouble keeping up, especially now the rocks were bigger and further apart.

'Come on!' Sonny called, his voice coming out in a loud gasp. 'They're gaining on us!'

Some of the boys looked back, knowing they wouldn't like what they saw. At the bottom of the rocks the ponies milled about, their bridles hanging. Writhing beneath the ponies, unseen and unfelt, were the wraiths, foaming at the edge of the hill.

Quickly they reached the start of the rocks and began to slide over, soon to catch up with Sonny and the other boys. Little Lou would be the first they touched.

'Faster!' Sonny tried to scream but he had screamed himself hoarse and could only gasp again. Little Lou started to falter and Sonny knew he wouldn't make it in time.

13.3 Writing in Stages: Middles

Here we are at the middle of your story. Now you should choose a specific event to work into what you already have.

This can be difficult but will always work in some way, even if you need to do a small re-write of what comes before. What you should remember is that stories are flexible and changeable and you have the power to do what you like with them.

When choosing your middle, if none of them seem to match then try to choose one which mirrors the feel or tone of your beginning. So if you have written something atmospheric and a bit spooky, you could choose *Eric felt a hand on his shoulder. He turned and a strange face was looking at him from behind the curtain.*

Eric, the curtain and the strange face might not exist in your beginning but they are creepy enough to become part of it if you have written something scary.

If all else fails, have something dramatic and surprising happen to link the start of your story to the middle. All you are looking for is an opportunity for the middle to join with your beginning.

Important!

You can change the names in these phrases to suit the characters in your own story. As long as the rest of the phrase stays the same, the name can be anything you like.

I have included an example to help you.

Middles

Clowns poured out of the side door of the theatre, screaming as the lion came after them.

'I change to suit myself,' Brian said, pulling on his jacket.

Eric felt a hand on his shoulder. He turned and a strange face was looking at him from behind the curtain.

The school creaked and groaned, the very structure succumbing to the giant space ship resting on the top of it.

The detective stepped over the pile of bodies on the floor and went to the window. It was his wife's birthday today.

A small tapping sound made Melody look up. There, in the window, a tiny bird pecked on the glass, looking at her inquisitively.

Janie walked away from the gym wishing she could stand up for herself sometimes. Why did she always give in and let people walk all over her? It was so unfair!

Candles lined the room, giving it a warm glow. As the door flew open, the cold, harsh wind rushed in and ravaged the flames, leaving all but one as smoking wicks.

Standing under the tree, he watched, unseen. Sooner or later they had to come out and when they did, he would be ready.

Babies were the worst things ever, Tanya thought, shuddering. She smiled sweetly as the Nursery Manager came over.

Example Middle

(For my example I have used *'I change to suit myself,' Brian said, pulling on his jacket).*

Lou hung back, his leg dragging and withered beneath him but still able to walk. He grasped fitfully at his jacket, trying to take it off to put on the overalls Sonny had found for them.

'Hurry up!' Sonny hissed, helping Lou with his jacket. He tried to drag it off carefully, unwilling to disturb the black grime which covered half of the younger boy's chest.

'I change to suit myself,' Brian said, pulling on his jacket. 'These outfits are stupid and nobody is going to be fooled, Sonny. There's no point!'

'There is every point if it keeps us alive for longer!' Sonny turned on him, suddenly fed up with Brian and his incessant whining. Lou shrank back, expecting them to fight and too shattered within and without to bear it.

13.4 Writing in Stages: Endings

Now we come to the end of your story. Even if you struggled with the middle, it could be harder than you think to round off your story when you have to use a prescribed ending.

Just like when you were choosing your middle, focus on the ending which matches the *feel* of your story as a whole, then work on the details later. Better to match the tone of your whole piece than to choose something simply for the sake of having an ending.

Like the beginnings, the endings are more vague so you should be able to blend them with your writing. Your choice from this section does not have to be written into the very end of your story; you could make it part of the final section, then end the story in your own way. Choose whichever method works best for you while including an option from this section.

Use my example to help you.

Endings

Ominously dark

Glitter paint spills

Funnily enough, they were lemmings

Crumbled and broke(n)

Biscuits everywhere

'No,' she spat

French doors to nowhere

A glance

Fragrance, like pepper

Fairy lights

Example Ending

(For my example I have used *Fragrance, like pepper*)

Lou crept over the top of the suitcases, careful as he could be not to dislodge them and give away his position. After everything they had been through, it all rested on him in the end. He wondered what might have happened if Brian hadn't pulled him away on the rocks – where would they be now?

Through no great heroics or plan, Lou was the one who could save them. It almost didn't matter, they had lasted longer than any of them expected. They were grateful for life, even if it only meant a few days more than when they first broke free.

A smell drifted down from above, caught in the dust motes dancing before him. A fragrance like pepper invaded his nose, exploring, tickling, teasing until he had to pause and hold a hand over his nostrils, waiting for the sneeze to pass.

There, gone and once again he had to move. Now that it had come to it, he hoped the numb acceptance would stand in for bravery and keep him going until the end.

14.1 The Klamarty Cave Creatures: Introduction

For as long as anyone can remember, the village of Klamarty has been quiet and rather dull. That all changed when locals found something strange in the Klamarty caves, down by the abandoned golf course. The caves are old and until recently were filled in with rubble and decades of debris.

Now they are being cleared out, ready to restart the golf course and bring new business to the village. The caves are not part of the golf course, but they are close by. The new owner of the golf course is Bob Cardigan, landlord of Twin Crows, the tiny local pub and he is the one who was clearing the caves.

Helping him were his step-son, Karl and his best friend Ludwig. Bob's wife, Suzette, was coming and going with snacks and drinks. All four of them were there when something strange happened...

Just as Ludwig took away the final barrow-load of debris and opened up the back of the first cave, a horrible wailing sound filled the air. Then a dark shape bolted past them, with what looked like a long tail flicking out behind it.

Ludwig ran, screaming and was followed by Suzette. Karl and Bob stood their ground, watching as the dark shape, moving too fast to make out, disappeared over the golf club fence and away. That was when they heard the squeaking noises from the back of the cave.

This is where the story seems to change, depending on who is telling it.

If you believe Bob and Karl, they found tiny, black baby creatures which look like a cross between a skinny cat and a lizard.

If you listen to Ludwig and Suzette, you will hear there are devils in the caves.

Some people in the village think that Bob and Karl are on a money-making scam and have made up the whole story and the devils are really just kittens.

Old Toby, who used to be the grounds-man at the golf course, says he has seen the tails of the baby creatures and they are definitely not kittens.

Bessy, Bob's neighbour, was washing her windows and just happened to be able to lean far enough to see into Bob's spare room and she said the so-called kittens were crawling on the walls.

Now the press have heard about the Klamarty Cave Creatures and they all want to know the truth about what Bob and his step-son found in the caves.

14.2 The Klamarty Cave Creatures: Different Stories: 1

Scenario

For this first set of tasks, you will need to write descriptively and persuasively. All the people involved want the press to listen their side of the story and some will exaggerate to be believed.

For each task, look at who the speaker is and what type of interview they are having. Some of the interviews are going to be **filmed**, so the finished story will be taken from what people are saying in real-life. Other interviews are going to be **read**. **Consider the difference** this would make to how you described the interviews.

Your task will be split into sections:

Writing to persuade

Choosing what will be included in the finished article and why

Writing or describing the finished article or news story

Different characters will use their own methods to persuade the interviewer they know the truth so pay attention to the personality and possible motives of each 'witness'.

Karl and Bob

Karl and Bob *plan* to offer a united front and tell the same story. They are interviewed together by Prina Grace of **CLO News**, a respected international news programme.

Task 1: The Statement

Write about what happened at the Caves, in Karl and/or Bob's words. You can either write this as dialogue (making is simpler to include both sides of their story) or as a descriptive piece.

Important! Karl and Bob are determined to persuade but desperately want to be taken seriously. They will be persuasive but they also want to keep their statements factual and not get carried away. They will present their statements as logical experience, even though they are describing something strange.

You should include:

What happened, from their point of view

A good description of the cave creatures

A reason they have not allowed other people to see the cave creatures since bringing them home

What they plan to do next with the creatures and the caves

What they think it will mean for the village

Here is a short example of what might be included in the Statement.

Example Statement

Bob: We ran in and there they were

Karl: Well, I ran in, you waited outside-

Bob: We found the babies and we knew they weren't normal

Karl: I said they were aliens

Bob: I knew we had to protect them

Karl: It was me who had to pick them all up though

Bob: We both carried them-

Karl: It was me who carried them

Bob: We took them home

Task 2: The Interviewer's Report

CLO News are here because this is a big story but in no way do they believe that Karl and Bob have found strange creatures in the caves. They will cover the story objectively and without stirring up any more excitement. They will stick to the facts and if Karl and Bob still refuse to show them the creatures, then they will limit the amount of time given to the story.

Write a short **report** based on what **Prina** thinks of the story. This should be descriptive and include opinions on the story itself, the people involved and decisions on what CLO will do with the finished story. Are there any important points which Prina might want to highlight for CLO bosses?

Look at the short example to see how this might be phrased.

Example Report

Lots of contradictions in the story, would be more useful to get Karl on his own but no chance with Bob around. Something odd going on so there's a mystery here. We should cover the story and see what we can dig up around the village, especially about Bob.

Task 3: The News Story

Based on what you have already written for this task, describe the finished news story, as it looks once it is released. You don't need to include every detail of what is said but you should mention anything that is left out or perhaps edited differently from how it was presented by Bob and Karl.

Look at how this short example compares with the others in this task.

Example News Story

In the middle of Bob's description of the creatures, the camera cuts to Karl's face and we see him look sceptical, as if he doesn't believe what his step-father is saying. When Karl speaks, the camera shows Bob smiling and nodding the whole time.

14.3 The Klamarty Cave Creatures: Different Stories: 2

Ludwig and Suzette

Ludwig and Suzette really want nothing to do with the strange creatures and dread the idea of them being out of the caves and loose in the village. Suzette hasn't been home since Bob brought the creatures into the spare room; she is staying at the pub until Bob comes to his senses and does something.

The pub is the venue for Ludwig and Suzette's interview with Mel Gamble from the **Crawler Times**, an internet site dedicated to all things strange and unexplained, in this world and any others.

Suzette would never normally give interviews but Ludwig is a fan of Crawler Times and has persuaded her to give just this one.

Task 1: The Statement

Ludwig and Suzette approach the interview in different ways. Ludwig wants to explain everything all at once, whereas Suzette takes a while to warm up and is still afraid.

Write about their interview and what they both say. You can write about their interview jointly or separately. Their stories will be **combined** on the Crawler Times website.

You should include:

Their specific descriptions of how the creatures look

Any extra details which support them thinking of the creatures as devils

Why they are both afraid of the creatures

What they think will happen next

What should happen to the creatures

Task 2: The Interviewer's Report

The Crawler Times may be a website which believes in all manner of strangeness but they are also proper journalists with a desire to find out the truth. Mel has no wish to be taken in by wild stories and he is a little suspicious of how eager Ludwig is to impress. However, he sees that Suzette is properly frightened by the whole ordeal and Mel is curious to find out more.

Write Mel's report which will be sent back to the editor of Crawler Times. Mel and the editor are friends so the report can be informal and full of opinions.

You should include:

His first impressions of Suzette and Ludwig

Whether he believes their story

What he thinks of the Klamarty Cave Creatures

How important or exciting he thinks the story might be for their website

Task 3: The News Story

Write Mel's article/story as it would appear on the Crawler Times. Think about the attitude and tone of his writing and how it might be presented to fans of this kind of website.

You should include:

How he sets the scene for the piece (would he describe the interview in the pub or a description of Klamarty Caves?)

How he describes the creatures

His own opinion on what the creatures might be

What he thinks will happen next

14.4 The Klamarty Cave Creatures: Different Stories: 3

The Local Newspaper

The story is not just an international mystery, it is also a very local one. The local newspaper, the Klamarty Times, is keen to cover the story and sell as many extra copies as it can. As well as newspaper articles, online and in print, they also feature mini-videos which appear alongside the news stories online. They usually focus on some element of the story, such as an important quote or a person who has vital information.

The Klamarty Times sends its best (and oldest) reporter out to cover the story. Clive Vernon is ready to retire and sick of being sent out to cover stupid stories while the younger reporters cover anything important. However, he's quite keen to visit Klamarty as his Uncle Toby used to be the grounds-man at the golf club and happens to know a back way into the caves…

Task: The Roving Reporter

Write a newspaper report from Clive's point of view. He will try to interview a few people to get a good feel for the story. Suzette is refusing to do any more interviews so Clive must see if the other people involved will speak to him.

He also interviews locals in the village, including his uncle Toby and Bessy, Bob's neighbour. Everyone has an opinion, so think about what people might say to him and what he would include and ignore.

You should also consider:

How many details are already known and whether Clive will repeat them or try for a different angle in his story

If he plans to visit the caves with Uncle Toby, how will this affect his writing? Eg will he include a clue that more information is to come? Will he plan to use this story as an introduction to the real one, written after his visit?

If Clive has an uncle in the village, will he also know any other people who are involved? How would this change his attitude to the story?

Has Clive himself ever been in the caves? Could this give him a personal angle on the story?

What would he choose to include as a mini-video to feature with his story?

14.5 The Klamarty Cave Creatures: What Happens Next?

Scenario

It is the end of the day and the village is quiet once more. **Karl** is at home, Suzette and Ludwig are at the pub, trying to persuade Bob to put the creatures back where he found them. Bob is enjoying having his pub full to overflowing but he pretends to consider what his wife and friend want him to do.

Mel, the reporter from the Crawler Times, has decided to do some investigating on his own and is camped out in Bob's front garden. He will wait until Karl goes to bed then he plans to go round the back, climb a ladder and look into the spare bedroom.

Clive and **Uncle Toby** are almost at the caves. They are working their way through the overgrown edge of the woods where a covered hole leads to the newly-revealed caves. Toby says Bob doesn't know about this back entrance as no one has used it for at least fifty years. As far as Toby remembers, it should come out in the cave where they found the creatures.

What Happens Next?

Now it is time to find out what happens next. Using the **Clues** below and the **Starter Lines** in each task, write about the Klamarty Cave Creatures.

You will be writing from the point of view of the people in each task, **Karl**, **Mel** and **Clive/Uncle Toby** – all their stories are happening at the same time, in different locations. For Clive and Uncle Toby you can use both their points of view or choose one as the dominant character.

Try to think how you might solve the mystery of the cave creatures, even if you are not sure what they are. The clues will help you to move the story along and your knowledge of the characters should mean you can work out what they might do.

You can leave the creatures a mystery in the end or you can resolve their story.

Clues

Look at the clues below and include at least one of them in each **Task**. You can use clues more than once as the events of each story happen at the same time.

A bright light, falling

Too many sounds, all at once

Suddenly, hammering

Obliterated, as if it never existed

A muggy smell, as if it had been locked up forever

Soft, like feathers

Then there it was, alone

The flowers were scattered everywhere

Digging, as if his life depended on it

Task 1: Karl's Story

Look at the starter lines below, choose a clue then write Karl's story.

Karl read the first lines of the book again, then threw it down. It was no good, he couldn't concentrate. He might as well go to bed.

As if throwing the book had disturbed them, he heard little feet scuttling about upstairs. He looked at the ceiling and sighed. Why did he have to be left in charge?

Then the scuttling became busier, madder, quicker and he heard the click of a door. They were out.

Task 2: Mel's Story

Look at the starter lines below, choose a clue then write Mel's story.

Mel shrugged off the leaves as they brushed his neck again. All this waiting, it was the worst part about being an investigator of strange phenomenon. He had no idea why unearthly creatures liked to make him wait in cold, dark places, but there it was.

A hand reached down onto his shoulder and he shrieked, briefly and girlishly, until he saw the concerned face of Bessy, the next door neighbour. She patted him to calm him down then whispered,

'I brought you a little dish of hot-pot. Thought you might need it.' She handed him a bowl wrapped in a cloth and smiled. 'Doing a stake out, I expect,' she added helpfully.

He looked at the bowl, wondering when his skills as a secretive investigator had deserted him. Before he could answer her, she looked to the house and said,

'What's that on the roof?'

Looking up, Mel saw a shape silhouetted against the half-moon sky.

Task 3: Clive and Uncle Toby's Story

Look at the starter lines below, choose a clue then write Clive and Uncle Toby's story.

Clive hoped he would be as fit as Toby when he was retired. They had ducked down into the awful hole in the ground and wandered along the passageway until it became too narrow. Now they crawled, Toby somehow covering ground faster than Clive could manage.

Just when Clive thought he could crawl no more and might like to sit for a bit and maybe have a drink, Toby stopped and waved a hand behind him. It was their signal for Clive to dim the light.

Clive fiddled with the torch-lantern thing Toby had given him and they were plunged into darkness. He gulped.

Toby moved again, slower this time and Clive hobbled after him, wondering if he could maybe sneak off back the way they had come without his uncle hating him forever.

A slim, sad light picked out the way in front of them and Clive realised it was the light from the opening at the cave entrance. They turned the final corner.

14.6 The Klamarty Cave Creatures: The Extra Moment

Task

To complete the story, choose one of the scenarios below and expand on it, making it part of your own, wider story. So, as well as writing more for the scenario, think of how you can link it with what you have written in the rest of this section.

Consider:

What details can you include to link the scenario with your own story?

Are there any characters from the rest of the section who can be included?

Could you make this extra part a real segment of your own story, such as a prologue or epilogue?

Do you need to change any details of your earlier story to make it fit together with this task?

Will you include an appearance by the cave creatures? Or a clue to the mystery which takes place in Klamarty?

Scenario 1

It is fifty years before the events in the rest of this section. Uncle Toby is a teenage boy who often gets into trouble and his father finds him a job at the golf course to show him the value of hard work. Instead, Toby spends his days sneaking off through the caves and hiding out in the woods on the other side so he does not have to work.

Scenario 2

On a cold night in February, an old dog goes missing in Klamarty village. No one notices until the next morning when he is found wandering on the golf course. His limp is better and he eats breakfast for the first time in three months.

Scenario 3

Finally, after all the hard work the golf course was busy again. The landscaped grounds shone in the sunshine, basking in warm weather.

Too much work and not enough time off in the sunshine, that's how young Lee saw it. What he really wanted was to have a sneaky rest and then maybe go off to the pub with his brother. He'd stop for a second and have a sly nap. Nobody would see him if he tucked himself inside the cave's entrance...

If you would like more creative writing ideas, visit www.amandajharrington.co.uk or www.creativewritingforkids.co.uk for news on creative writing courses with feedback and free books.

You might also like:

Printed in Poland
by Amazon Fulfillment
Poland Sp. z o.o., Wrocław